I WAITED UNTIL ALL THE LIGHTS WERE OUT AND EVERYONE WAS ASLEEP.

Then I quietly got dressed and slipped out of my room. Nebula was waiting for me.

I switched my data pad to 3-D mode, and a map of the United States floated before us.

"Here's where we are now," I told her, pointing to a spot on the map just outside of New York City. "And here's where we want to go."

My finger moved toward Cleveland, Ohio. Nebula did not look happy.

"This is where the Thirty-Fourth Annual World Science Fair is being held," I continued. "Tomorrow is my last chance to enter my Galaxy Glue."

Zenon's stories are stellar!
Look who says so . . .

Don't miss these other Zenon stories!

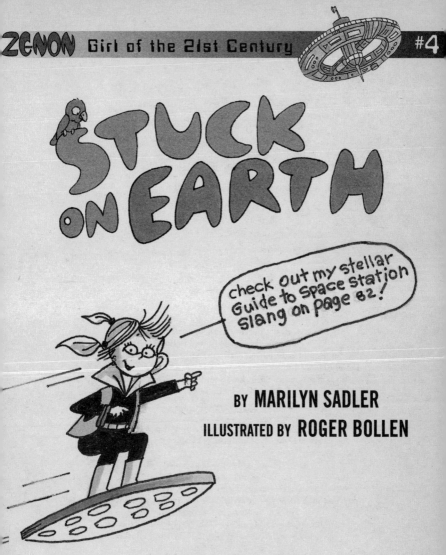

STUCK ON EARTH

check out my stellar Guide to Space Station slang on page 82!

BY **MARILYN SADLER**

ILLUSTRATED BY **ROGER BOLLEN**

A Stepping Stone Book™

Random House 🏠 New York

Text copyright © 2002 by Marilyn Sadler
Illustrations copyright © 2002 by Roger Bollen
All rights reserved under International and Pan-American Copyright Conventions.
Published in the United States of America by Random House Children's Books,
a division of Random House, Inc., New York, and simultaneously in Canada
by Random House of Canada Limited, Toronto.

www.randomhouse.com/kids

Library of Congress Cataloging-in-Publication Data
Stuck on Earth / by Marilyn Sadler ; illustrated by Roger Bollen.
p. cm. —
(Zenon, girl of the 21st century ; #4)
"A stepping stone book."
SUMMARY: Zenon and Nebula, of Space Station 9, need help from an Earth boy
when they sneak away from a class field trip to enter Zenon's Galaxy Glue in the
34th Annual World Science Fair in Cleveland.
ISBN 0-679-89252-4 (trade) — ISBN 0-679-99252-9 (lib. bdg.)
[1. Science—Exhibitions—Fiction. 2. School field trips—Fiction.
3. Glue—Fiction. 4. Science fiction.]
I. Bollen, Roger, ill. II. Title. III. Series. PZ7.S1239 St 2002 [Fic]—dc21 2001048976

Printed in the United States of America First Edition June 2002 10 9 8 7 6 5 4 3 2

CONTENTS

1
GALAXY GLUE

"I have a surprise for you today, class!" said my teacher early one Monday morning.

My best friend and I had just walked into our classroom at Quantum Elementary. A 3-D globe of Earth was spinning slowly in the middle of the room.

What in the name of Neptune is Mr. Peres up to now? I wondered as Nebula and I slipped into our seats.

I did not have to wait long for an answer.

"We are traveling to Earth on a field trip!" cried Mr. Peres. "Pack your bags tonight, because we leave first thing in the morning!"

I felt my face flare up like a Pandorian sunset. This was the inkiest thing he could have told us. I'd rather float in space without a jet-pack than go to Earth!

Earth was a universe away from the Mars

Malt, my favorite chill chamber on Space Station 9. Gravity was a scorch. It made me feel as heavy as a Lootar. And big skies and wide-open spaces made me dizzy.

I was completely shivered out. But Mr. Peres didn't seem to notice.

"We will be traveling to a small town outside of New York City," he continued. "My good friend teaches at a school there, and he has agreed to be our host. Then we will visit the United States capital, Washington, D.C.!"

My classmates cheered as I slumped farther down in my seat. There I remained, in a Martian mist, for the rest of the day.

That night, I sat down at my data pad to look up Earth. I needed to find at least *one* good reason to go on this inky field trip.

I had just started my search when Nebula blasted into my room.

"Thermo!" she said as a large picture of Earth appeared on my data pad screen.

It did not take long to find a few good things about Earth. There was a Rock and Roll Hall of Fame. There were hyperspeed trains. There was the Moons of Jupiter amusement park. But other than that, there was nothing worth going quasar over.

Then something caught my eye.

It was an announcement. The Thirty-Fourth Annual World Science Fair was about to be held in Cleveland, Ohio. First prize was fifty thousand frackles.

"Ceedus-Lupeedus!" I cried as I felt geezle bumps travel up my arms.

You're probably wondering why I got so excited about a science fair. Most girls my age think science is inky. Well, cool your boosters because I'm about to tell you.

I, Zenon Kar, have *always* loved science.

In fact, I had just won the Fifth Annual Quantum Elementary School Science Fair with an invention of mine called Galaxy Glue.

I had been looking forward to the Fifth Annual Quantum Elementary School Science Fair ever since the Fourth Annual Quantum Elementary School Science Fair had ended.

That was the year I lost to my friend Tad. He had invented a paint that changed colors when he told it to.

"Stellar Yellow," he had said to a painted white wall behind the judges.

The judges gasped in surprise when the wall turned from white to yellow right before their eyes.

After that, I wanted to dazzle the judges, too. So I began to work on my Galaxy Glue.

At first, my glue was nothing more than your ordinary mucky paste. It caused paper to stick to paper. And paper to stick to metal or glass.

As you well know, that is nothing new. I wanted my glue to cause things to stick together that had *never* stuck together before. And if you've never tried to do it, let me tell you, it isn't easy making things stick together when they don't want to be stuck.

Then one night, I had a major break-through.

I was working on my glue in my room. My robotic dog, Bobo, was asleep at my side. I had just taken a sip of a Whambama Smoothie. Then my dad knocked on my door.

Bobo woke with a start. He knocked my smoothie out of my hand. It fell into my glue. And the glue began to bubble and foam.

I tried to pick up the Zarkon metal cup that my Whambama Smoothie had been in. But it was stuck to my Calzon glass tabletop.

Whambama was the missing ingredient. It was what I had been searching for!

I added whambama to my formula. And suddenly my glue could make *anything* stick to *anything*! It was thermo beyond belief!

When it was time for the science fair, *I* was the one to dazzle the judges. And I won first place.

Now here I was, staring at my data-pad screen and the announcement for the Thirty-Fourth Annual World Science Fair. *This* was my chance to show my glue to the *world*!

"That science fair is for adults," said Nebula, bringing me back to reality. "Mr. Peres will say no."

It was true. Mr. Peres would never let me enter my glue in an adult science fair.

"So I just won't ask him," I decided.

Nebula's eyes lit up like solar flares.

"You mean you would sneak off to the fair without permission?" asked Neb.

That was exactly what I meant.

"But the fair is in Cleveland, Ohio, Zee!" Nebula tried again. "We're not going to Cleveland."

I did not see that this was a problem either. There were superfast trains on Earth.

I punched up the hyperspeed-train schedule on my data pad.

"Traveling to Cleveland from Washington, D.C., on a hyperspeed train takes two hours. That's no more time than it takes to ride twice around Space Station 9," I told Neb.

But Neb did not want to hear it.

"Something could go wrong," she said. "You could get kidnapped or lost!"

"You're being a Plutar Blanchy!" I told her, shaking my head.

But Neb still wasn't listening.

"Worse yet, you could get *stuck* on Earth!" was the last thing she said as she walked out the door.

2
ONE-TRAIN-TRACK MIND

The next morning, my parents took me to the departure port. My class was already boarding the shuttle when we arrived.

"Bye, Mom! Bye, Dad!" I said, and hugged them both.

They knew how scorched-out I was about traveling to Earth, so Mom gave me a few extra frackles for my trip.

"Treat yourself to something special," she whispered as she slipped the coins into my pocket.

I found Nebula sitting by a window toward the back of the shuttle. I hurried over to join her.

"Hey, Neb!" I said, and slid into the seat next to her.

"Hey, Zee!" she cried with a quasar smile.

She no longer seemed flared-up about the science fair. So I decided not to mention it.

Once the flight took off, Mr. Peres began to lecture us. He didn't even cool his boosters when the shuttle stewards served our lunch!

"We live in an enclosed area on Space Station 9," he said. "When you arrive on Earth, you may be uncomfortable with the big sky and the wide-open spaces."

Mr. Peres swept his hand out from his side when he said this. I guess he was making a point about the wide-open spaces. But he knocked my drink out of my hand and into my bowl of Jupiter Jell-O.

"Ceedus-Lupeedus!" I whispered. He was driving me into hyperspace!

I watched as my Pluto Punch swirled around in my Jell-O and began to bubble and foam. It made me think of the night my life was changed forever. The night I spilled the Whambama Smoothie into my Galaxy Glue.

For the rest of the trip, I could not concentrate on Mr. Peres's lecture. I imagined myself winning fifty thousand frackles at the Thirty-Fourth Annual World Science Fair.

When we finally touched down on Earth, my classmates started to cheer. I sat there in silence, looking out the window. The sight of all those trees really scorched me out.

I stepped off the ramp and the gravity hit me like a ton of Zarkon metal. I could barely lift my feet as I walked across the runway.

The Earth shuttle port was much larger than the port on the space station. There were crowds of people everywhere! They looked strange in their silly hats and Earth clothing.

We might as well have landed on Fenebula.

Mr. Peres hurried us aboard a hyperspeed train. We sped out of the station and into the countryside. In no time, we arrived at the Shady Pines Inn, just outside of New York City.

To my horror, there were pine trees everywhere. They smelled funny, and their needles were all over the ground.

"Jumping Jupiter!" I screamed when one of the needles poked through my space shoes. "If it weren't for this stupid gravity, I'd be able to pick up my feet, instead of shuffling along like a Lootar!"

The first few days of our trip, Mr. Peres kept us very busy. He took us to Lincoln Elementary School, where we sat in on some of the classes.

I could not believe that the windows were open in every room.

How were you supposed to concentrate?

There were birds chirping outside. And the flowers and trees made half my class sneeze.

It didn't matter, though. I couldn't focus on anything but my secret plans.

The first chance I got, I slipped away from my classmates. In the Earth school's library, I found a map of the United States. I charted the course to Cleveland. I stored the information on my data pad.

That night, we went to a football game to watch the Tigers play the Falcons. I watched for a while, but I lost interest. It was nothing like my favorite game—spaceball. I mean, football is okay, but how can you get excited about a game played entirely on the *ground*?

At halftime, Mr. Peres gave each of us a few frackles for refreshments.

I didn't buy any popcorn or peanuts. Instead, I shoved the coins deep in my pocket. Added to the extra frackles my mom had given me, they would be enough to buy two train tickets to Cleveland.

While my classmates watched the end of the game, I searched the sky for Space Station 9. I thought I saw it. But Mr. Peres said I was looking at the North Star.

I was happy when the game was finally over. It was too *cold* on Earth to be outside!

The next day, Mr. Peres took us to a farm so we could see how food was produced.

Farming on Earth is much harder than on the space station. On Space Station 9, we control our weather. But on Earth, it either rains too much or too little. It's either too hot or too cold.

The whole planet should be under a dome! I decided.

After a tour of the fields and barns, the farmer's wife served us ham sandwiches and corn. I helped myself to extra sandwiches. Then I hid them in my backpack for the trip to Cleveland!

At the end of the day, I was feeling pretty thermo. All my secret plans were falling into place. I couldn't wait to share them with Nebula.

That night at dinner, Mr. Peres made an announcement.

"Tomorrow, we will see what life is like in the city," he said. "At eleven o'clock sharp, we will be taking the hyperspeed train from here to the capital of the United States, Washington, D.C.!"

All my classmates cheered.

After dinner, Mr. Peres lectured for hours about the history of Washington. He showed us a digital movie about the White House and the Capitol building. Finally, he dismissed us. All the kids were yawning. It was very late, almost midnight, and they were ready for bed.

Me, I had a different idea.

"Meet me in an hour behind the inn," I whispered in Nebula's ear.

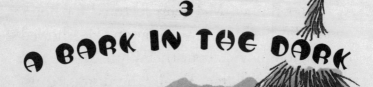

3
A BARK IN THE DARK

I waited until all the lights were out and everyone was asleep. Then I quietly got dressed and slipped out of my room.

When I got to the back of the inn, Nebula was waiting for me. She was sitting at a picnic table under a large pine tree. Her eyes were as big as the moons of Jupiter.

"What's blasting?" she asked before I could sit down.

I didn't say a word as I switched my data pad to 3-D mode. Within seconds, a map of the United States appeared, floating before us.

Nebula stared at it with a scorchy look on her face. I knew she was on to me.

"Here's where we are now," I told her, pointing to a spot on the map just outside of New York City. "And here's where we want to go."

My finger moved toward Cleveland, Ohio. I looked over at Nebula. She did not look happy.

"This is where the Thirty-Fourth Annual World Science Fair is being held," I said. "Tomorrow is my last chance to enter my Galaxy Glue."

I moved my hand away from the map and sat down. Nebula stared at Cleveland for a long time. Then, finally, she looked at me.

"When do we leave?" she asked.

I knew there was a reason Neb was my best friend!

"According to my calculations, if we leave now, we'll have more than enough time. First we'll take the hyperspeed train to Cleveland. Then we'll enter my Galaxy Glue in the Science Fair at seven o'clock in the morning, when they open. And finally we'll be back by ten in the morning to leave at eleven for Washington!"

Nebula liked my plan. And there was a good chance that Mr. Peres wouldn't even miss us.

"So let's blast out of here!" she said.

Nebula followed me as I set out for the train station. We'd had to travel outside of the city to get to the Shady Pines Inn when we first arrived. So I thought I knew the way back into town.

But before long, we were lost.

I pointed my laser lamp down the dark path. Nothing looked familiar.

It was so frustrating!

On the space station, I could easily find my way around. The halls were named and numbered. But along a country lane on Earth, *nothing* was labeled. How in the name of Neptune were you supposed to tell one inky tree from another?

Then, all of a sudden, there was a loud hooting sound. Nebula and I hit the ground and covered our heads with our hands.

The noise was coming from one of the trees. I pointed my laser lamp in that direction. Sitting on a high limb was a bird with huge eyes.

"I think that's an owl," whispered Nebula.

"Are they dangerous?" I asked.

Nebula did not know. She had seen a picture of an owl in the Earth school we had visited. But she had not learned anything about it.

We decided to look it up on my data pad. So I punched in *O-W-L* and began to read.

". . . a night bird having a large head, large eyes, and a short, hooked beak. It feeds on children lost in the woods after dark. . . ."

At that, Neb screamed at the top of her lungs and took off running!

I did not have a chance to tell her that I had made a mistake. I had read a description from the movie *Attack of the Killer Owls*.

When I caught up with Neb, she was hiding under a bush at the end of the road.

"I'm sorry!" I cried. I explained what I had done.

We were both shivered-out and a little bit nervous. Neither of us thought my mistake was funny.

Earth is as dark as a black hole, I thought.

With a sigh, I got back on the path. Neb followed.

After a few steps, my laser lamp flashed on the eyes of an animal. It let out a bark as Neb and I started screaming. I dropped my lamp, and we took off running again.

Neb and I ran until we were out of breath. Then we fell to the ground, gasping for air. Lying in the dark, I felt like I was about to go lunar.

"Are you all right, Neb?" I asked in a shaky voice.

We were barely into our adventure and were already in global meltdown.

"I think so," she said, breathing hard. "What do we do now?"

I sat up and looked around. We were lost. We had no light. And it was as dark as deep space.

Then something in the distance caught my eye. "Look, Neb!" I cried, pointing.

Neb sat up.

There was a barn at the end of a field. And there was a light on inside it. It was the only light in a world of darkness.

"Maybe there's someone in there who can help us," I said, and jumped to my feet.

4
BENNY GONZALEZ

I raced through the dark field. Nebula followed close behind me.

When we got to the barn door, I slowly pushed it open and peered inside, where I saw a young boy brushing a horse.

When the boy saw us, he put down his brush.

"I know you," he said. "You're from the space station. You visited my school."

Neb and I remembered him, too. His name was Benny Gonzalez. He had led our class through Lincoln School during our tour.

"It's stellar to see you again!" I said, shaking his hand.

Benny studied us for a moment. I knew he was wondering what we were doing in his barn.

Then he asked, "Why aren't you back at the Shady Pines Inn?"

"We got lost on the way to the train station," I said.

"You must have turned the wrong way," he said. "The station's just a mile past Lincoln Elementary on the left."

Benny told us he'd been sleeping. But something had spooked his horse, so he'd gotten up, gotten dressed, and come to the barn to calm it down.

Then he sort of squinted at both of us. I suppose he had just figured out *who* had spooked his horse.

But he didn't seem to mind. With a smile, he said, "Why don't I take you to the train station?"

Neb and I were happy to let him. We followed him out of the barn.

There were eyes everywhere in the dark. I knew they were animals. But to me they looked like Blotozoid Zombies. I tried not to look and kept my eyes focused on Benny instead.

He took us along the same path back toward town. This time, however, Neb and I weren't inked-out. We felt safe with this boy from Earth.

Benny led us across a large bog. He said it was a shortcut to town. But the ground was wet and muddy.

Our space station shoes were made for metal floors. They were not made for wet grass and mud.

Pwuck, pwuck, they sounded as Neb and I
struggled with every step.

I didn't understand how anyone could live
on this scorchy planet. It was muddy. It was
dark. It was downright spooky.

When we finally saw the lights of town, I
was so happy. Neb and I hurried toward the
main street, and for a moment, Benny was
following *us*.

We turned left at the center of town and hurried past Lincoln Elementary. Before long, the train station came into view.

Benny took us inside. There were very few people catching trains that night. It was late—*very* late!—and everyone was home sleeping.

He asked where we were going, and we told him. Then he helped us check the schedule to Cleveland at the ticket window. There was a train leaving in one hour.

"When are you coming back?" Benny asked.

"Tomorrow morning," I said. "Before ten."

We had to get back before Mr. Peres missed us!

Benny thought for a moment as he studied the train schedule. Then he turned toward us.

"Can I come, too?" he asked. "I've always wanted to see the Rock and Roll Hall of Fame. I heard it stays open all night."

Neb and I looked at each other in surprise. I knew what she was thinking. She was thinking it would be thermo to have this Earth boy along on our trip.

5
THE MYSTERY MAN

"We'd love to have you come with us, Benny!" I told him. "But what about your parents? Won't they miss you?"

"My parents are in Mexico," said Benny. "I live with my uncle."

Benny's uncle was a farmer. The barn we had found Benny in was his uncle's.

"He leaves to work the fields before I get up in the morning," said Benny. "He doesn't come back until it's dark."

Benny's uncle wouldn't miss him. We would be back from Cleveland long before he returned from the fields.

Benny smiled and stepped up to the ticket counter.

"Make that *three* tickets to Cleveland," he said to the clerk.

With our tickets in hand, Neb, Benny, and I waited for the train. Neb and I actually fell asleep on a bench, but Benny woke us up just as the train was about to leave.

We found three seats in front of a man who was sitting alone. As I sat down, I smiled at him. He did not smile back.

I thought that was inky. But as the train began to pull out of the station, I forgot about him.

A few minutes later, we were flying through the countryside at lightning speed.

"I can't look out the window!" I cried to Benny, covering my eyes. "It makes me dizzy!"

Benny laughed at me. He must have thought I was the most lunar girl in the universe!

I looked at my watch. It was way, *way* past midnight. Almost four in the morning! Neb and I had left the Shady Pines Inn hours ago!

No wonder I'm hungry, I thought as I reached into my backpack for something to eat. I was glad I had packed the ham sandwiches from our trip to the farm.

Nebula had fallen asleep. So Benny and I hungrily ate our sandwiches. When we were finished eating, we were both wide awake and ready to talk.

"Why are you going to Cleveland, anyway?" Benny asked me.

I had been so busy trying to get to the train station that I had almost forgotten why we were going. Now that we were on our way, I was quasar with excitement!

"I invented a glue," I told Benny, "that will make *anything* stick to *anything*!"

I reached into my backpack and pulled out my jar of Galaxy Glue. Then I handed it to Benny.

"The only reason it doesn't stick to the jar is because the inside of the jar is coated with a nonstick Flooton plastic," I explained.

Benny shook my jar of glue and turned it over and over in his hands.

"I won a science fair back home on the space station," I said. "We're going to Cleveland so I can enter my glue in the Thirty-Fourth Annual World Science Fair. The prize is fifty thousand frackles!"

Benny looked up at me. His eyes were lit up like solar flares. I was happy to see how excited he was.

"That's so thermo!" he cried. "Do you think you can win?"

I was certain I could win. No one had ever been able to stick Zarkon metal to Calzon glass before.

"I think I have a very good chance," I told him.

Benny handed me back my jar of glue. As I slipped it into my backpack, I noticed that the man behind me was leaning forward.

He had been listening to every word I said!

I decided to turn around and say hello. But when I did, he just turned away.

Is this how Earth adults act? I wondered.

In the name of Neptune, I did not know.

6
BROKEN DREAMS

I was so shivered-out by the inky man behind me that I didn't talk the rest of the two-hour trip. Benny did not understand why I was so quiet. But if I tried to explain, the man would hear me.

Benny soon got tired and fell asleep. Neb was still asleep, so I had no one to talk to.

I couldn't look out the window without getting dizzy. And the man behind me was staring at me. At least, I thought I could feel his eyes on the back of my neck.

I was never so happy to see the sun when it finally appeared in the sky. It was rising over a huge lake. I had never seen so much water in one place in all my life.

I woke up Nebula and Benny.

"Look at that!" I said to them, pointing out at the water.

"That's Lake Erie," said Benny, yawning, not the least bit surprised.

I had almost forgotten this was his planet.

"It's one of the five Great Lakes," he said.

43

I couldn't believe there were five of them like this one. No wonder they called them the *Great* Lakes. They were cosmic.

Just then, the train turned south, and a large city came into view. I tried to look at it more closely, but the train was moving too fast.

"Next stop, Cleveland, Ohio!" shouted the conductor.

"We're here!" I cried.

Nebula and I gathered up our backpacks as the train pulled into the station. I looked out the window. It was six o'clock in the morning, and the station was already bustling with people.

I took one last look at the inky man

behind us and gave him a scorchy stare. Then I hurried off after my friends.

We marched straight to the information counter and got directions to the science fair. It was close enough that we could walk. So we hiked out of the station.

Poor Neb hadn't eaten anything all night. I gave her a ham sandwich. She gobbled it right up.

Cleveland was stellar! There were trains and cars and boats and planes. I was definitely a *city* girl, I decided. Cities were much more like space stations than country towns were.

When we got to the science fair, it was just opening its doors for the day. I was so excited, I thought I'd go lunar.

There was a huge banner on the side of the science center. It read:

WELCOME TO THE 34TH ANNUAL WORLD SCIENCE FAIR

"This is it!" I shouted.

It was a dream come true. I couldn't believe I had made it all the way from Space Station 9 to Cleveland, Ohio! It was stellar beyond belief!

Then, all of a sudden, I felt someone tugging on my backpack! I spun around to look.

"*Ceedus-Lupeedus!*" I cried.

It was the inky man from the train!

"He's after my glue!" I shouted, holding on to my backpack with all my might. I wasn't going to let go for all the stardust in the galaxy.

When he heard me scream, Benny turned and raced toward us. The man panicked and let go of my backpack. It plunked down to the ground in front of me.

I heard the sound of breaking glass. Galaxy Glue came oozing out of my backpack. It spread on the pavement all around my feet.

I looked up at Nebula.

"My glue!" I cried.

7

A CLUE TO THE GLUE

Nebula reached for the broken jar of glue. I knew she wanted to help me. But I had to stop her.

"Don't touch the glue!" I shouted.

Nebula looked up at me in confusion.

"You'll get *stuck*, Neb!" I told her.

As I said that, I looked down at my feet. The glue had formed a puddle around me. I tried to pick up my space shoes. But they would not budge.

The glue had seeped through my shoes and socks, which meant . . .

My feet were glued to my socks. My socks were glued to my shoes. And my shoes were glued to the *ground*!

"That was all the glue I had!" I said as tears welled up in my eyes. I would no longer be able to enter the science fair.

Neb and I stood in silence. We did not know what to do. We were both shivered-out beyond belief.

Then, as if things couldn't get any scorchier, Benny ran off. He left us when we needed him most!

"All Earth people are inky!" I said.

Nebula threw her arms around me, and we started to cry.

Our trip to Earth was a total disaster!

"Look!" shouted Nebula suddenly.

I turned my head. To my surprise, Benny was walking toward us. With him was a tall, thin man with glasses.

"I'd like you to meet Albert Geezle," said Benny when they reached us. "Mr. Geezle is the great-grandson of the famous inventor Alfred Geezle. He is also the man in charge of the science fair."

I could not believe my ears! Alfred Geezle was my hero. Next to the singer Proto Zoa and my dad, he was the most thermo man in the universe.

"It is stellar to meet you," I said, going quasar with excitement.

Mr. Geezle had a kind face. I could tell that he wanted to help me. So I quickly told him what had happened. When I was finished, he shook his head.

"That man wanted to steal *your* glue and enter it in *my* science fair!" he said angrily.

I was happy that Mr. Geezle was flared-up about the inky man. But at this point, I was more worried about my glue.

"What should I do now?" I asked him.

Mr. Geezle looked down at the glue around my feet. It had dried and hardened. When he bent down to touch it, I did not stop him.

"Is there anything special about this glue I should know?" he asked me, knocking on it with his knuckles.

I did not want to give away my glue's secret ingredient. But I knew that I had to tell him if I wanted him to help me.

"Yes, sir," I said. "It has whambama in it."

Mr. Geezle looked up at me. He seemed very surprised.

"Wait here," he said as he hurried off toward the science center.

A short time later, Mr. Geezle returned with a small group of men and women.

"These are some of the best scientists on Earth," he explained to me. "They are here for the Thirty-Fourth Annual World Science Fair. They may be able to help us."

The scientists introduced themselves to me. They were very interested in my glue. They chipped off samples of it and asked me questions. They were looking for any clues that might help them.

"What is *whambama*?" they wanted to know.

This was the first time I realized they did not grow whambama on Earth. It was probably too hot or cold . . . or too wet or dry.

The space station must be the only place whambama is grown, I thought.

"It's a berry-like fruit," I explained. "It's made from bananas, pineapples, and kiwi."

"Hmmm," they all muttered, deep in thought.

I wondered what they were thinking, but they didn't say a word. They didn't even talk to each other.

They finished chipping. Then they took their samples and left just as quickly as they had come.

I looked over at Mr. Geezle. He seemed more worried than ever.

"We can only hope that the scientists come up with something to dissolve your glue, Zenon," he said, "or you may be stuck here for a *very* long time."

8
THE GLUE'S IN THE NEWS

Mr. Geezle excused himself. Then he followed the scientists back into the science center.

He had inked me out cosmically. I didn't want to stay stuck in Cleveland. My parents would miss me. I had school to attend. And what about my friends?

My stellar plans had come unglued.

I just wished my feet would.

Nebula began to pace in front of me. She was worried about Mr. Peres. Our class would be leaving for Washington, D.C., in a few hours—and we would not be there to join them.

"Maybe I'd better call him," said Neb, coming to a stop in front of me.

I hated to think of telling Mr. Peres what I had done. But I knew Nebula was right.

"Tell him that some of the best scientists on Earth are working on it," I said as she turned to go.

Nebula ran off toward the science center to use the phones. I was left alone with Benny.

"Don't worry," he said, putting his arm around me. "You'll be back home on Space Station 9 before you know it."

I was deep in thought about home when, to my surprise, Mr. Geezle came running back toward us. He had a quasar smile on his face.

"I have great news!" he cried.

I was sure the scientists had found a solution to my problem. But I was wrong.

"We caught the man who tried to steal your glue," said Mr. Geezle. "He was stuck in front of the Rock and Roll Hall of Fame! He must have stepped in some of your glue when the jar broke."

I was happy that the inky man was caught. But it did not solve my problem.

Then, all of a sudden, a bright light flashed in my face.

I looked up to see a woman standing in front of me. To her side was a man holding a camera. It was pointed right at me.

"I'm a reporter from WKYC," the woman said. She pushed a microphone in front of my face. "May I ask you some questions?"

I had nothing else to do, and certainly nowhere to go. So I agreed to talk to her.

"Tell me about your Galaxy Glue," she said.

I was surprised that she knew about my glue. I hadn't told anyone but Mr. Geezle and the scientists. News traveled fast on Earth. Soon the whole planet would know.

I explained what Galaxy Glue was and what it could do. I told her how it could make Zarkon metal stick to Calzon glass.

I thought I had told her everything she needed to know. Then she scorched me out with her next question.

"Why did you use whambama?" she asked.

Whambama was my secret ingredient! No

one was supposed to know about it but Mr. Geezle and the scientists!

What a bunch of blabberbabbles! I thought.

"I used whambama because the juice of the banana, pineapple, and kiwi gave my glue the sticking power it needed," I said.

The reporter seemed happy with my answer. She asked the cameraman to take a close-up of my feet. He pointed his camera down at the pavement, where my space shoes were surrounded by glue. Then he pointed the camera at my face.

Meanwhile, a huge crowd of people had gathered around me. They were taking pictures and asking questions. Other scientists had stopped to see me as well.

I heard someone say that there were more people *outside* the science center than there were *inside*.

Ceedus-Lupeedus! I had become the main attraction at the science fair!

Back on the space station, my parents had just finished dinner. They went into the living room to watch the Space Station 9 evening news.

The main story that night was from Earth. My mom and dad were very interested. After all, their daughter was on Earth with her class for a field trip.

What they did not expect was that their daughter *was* the main story.

"A young girl who traveled to Earth from Space Station 9 for the Thirty-Fourth Annual World Science Fair may *not* be coming home soon," said the reporter. "It seems she is stuck on Earth."

9
SCIENCE TRIUMPHS

My parents went supernova when my face suddenly appeared on their 3D-TV screen.

"*Zenon!*" cried my mother in surprise.

The reporter from WKYC explained what had happened to me. My parents sat in shock while they listened carefully to every word.

They didn't know that I was traveling to Cleveland, Ohio. They didn't know that I was entering a science fair. They didn't even know that I had taken my Galaxy Glue with me on my field trip.

"What *else* didn't she tell us?" asked my father, getting more flared-up by the minute.

When the news story was over, my parents flew out the door like two comets on fire. They raced to the departure port. Then they caught the next shuttle to Cleveland.

"That girl is going to drive me into hyperspace," said my mother, shaking her head.

Back on Earth, the crowd around me had grown larger. I was surprised that so many people were interested in me. I was beginning to feel like a superstar.

I no longer cared about the science fair. I no longer cared about winning fifty thousand frackles. I had shown my Galaxy Glue to the world, and everybody loved it!

I didn't stay quasar for long, however.

Over the heads of the crowd, I saw a scorchy face coming toward me. It was my teacher, Mr. Peres. His face was as red as a Pandorian sunset.

Mr. Peres and my class had just arrived on the hyperspeed train from New York. They had received Neb's phone call as they were leaving for Washington, D.C. They had made a quick change of plans. And now here they were, in Cleveland.

At first, Mr. Peres stopped when he saw the crowd of people gathered around me. Then he lit up like a solar flare and pushed his way through.

When he reached me, I could tell that he was not about to cool his boosters.

"Zenon Kar, I am very disappointed in you," he said sternly. "You left Shady Pines without my permission."

I could hear my classmates snickering in the background. They had followed Mr. Peres through the crowd. Now they were standing behind him, laughing and pointing at my feet.

"I'm sorry, Mr. Peres," I said, looking down. "I just wanted to enter my glue in the Thirty-Fourth Annual World Science Fair."

Mr. Peres did not approve of my answer. He stared at me like the inky man on the train.

"I have half a mind to leave you stuck on Earth," he said.

I thought I was going to be swallowed up by a black hole!

Stuck on Earth! I couldn't think of an inkier fate!

I wanted to go *home*. I missed the brightly lit halls of my space station. I missed the sound of my space shoes on Zarkon metal floors. I missed the unchanging temperature and enclosed spaces.

Then, as if things weren't scorchy enough, I saw my parents. They were pushing their way through the crowd. Mom was in global meltdown. And Dad was wearing his stress reducer.

I no longer felt like a stellar twenty-first-century inventor. Suddenly I felt like a big Pandorian Lootar. I was stuck in my Galaxy Glue for the entire universe to see.

"Ceedus-Lupeedus," I muttered under my breath. "What next?"

My dad broke through the crowd in front of me. He opened his mouth to speak. Then, all of a sudden, a loud noise came from the science center. Someone was shouting.

Everyone turned to look.

Running toward us was the group of scientists I had met earlier in the day—the best scientists on Earth. One of them was carrying a large jar.

"We've got it!" he called, to everyone's amazement. "We've got the mixture that will dissolve your glue, Zenon Kar!"

10
A MICROBE MOMENT

Everyone stepped back. The scientists formed a circle around me. They all took one last look at the glue that had hardened around my feet. Then they opened their mixture and poured it over my Galaxy Glue.

My glue began to bubble and foam. It turned purple, then blue.

Everyone watched in silence.

Slowly, I picked up one of my feet and set it down outside the puddle. Then I lifted my other foot and walked a few steps away.

"I'm free!" I cried.

The crowd burst into cheers!

It was stellar beyond belief!

"Thank you!" I said to the scientists with all my heart. "Now I can go home."

Mom and Dad blasted over and hugged me. They were no longer flared-up now that I was in their arms. But I still felt like a Pandorian Lootar.

"I'm so sorry," I said with tears in my eyes. "I know I did an inky thing."

Mom and Dad agreed. They were very disappointed in me. But they thought I'd learned my lesson.

"Being stuck on Earth is almost punishment enough," said my mom.

"*Almost*," added my dad. "But we'll discuss that when we get home."

Albert Geezle and all the judges from the science fair had arrived just in time to see me unglued. They were very proud of the scientists. They shook their hands and congratulated them.

Then Albert Geezle made an important announcement.

"We have chosen the winner of the Thirty-Fourth Annual World Science Fair!" he said. "Or should I say *winners?*"

The crowd gasped in surprise.

The judges did something they had never done before. They gave the first-place award of fifty thousand frackles to more than one person. They gave it to all the scientists who had created the mixture to dissolve Galaxy Glue.

"Advances in science are not always made by one person working alone," said Albert Geezle. "If it had not been for these scientists working together, this young girl might have been stuck on Earth forever."

At that, everyone turned and looked at me.

Then they began to applaud.

I didn't know if they were clapping for me or for the scientists. But I didn't care. I was going home.

"Are you ready?" asked my dad, putting his arm around me.

I couldn't *wait* to get back to Space Station 9. But there was one thing I had to do first.

I spotted Benny Gonzalez in the crowd.

He was talking to some of my classmates. I excused myself. I walked over to Benny, took his hand, and led him over to my parents.

"Mom and Dad," I said, "I want you to meet my new friend, Benny Gonzalez. If it weren't for him, we'd still be lost in the woods in New York."

I could tell from the looks on my parents' faces that this was a story for another time. They had been shivered-out enough for one day.

Just as we had promised, Neb and I took Benny to the Rock and Roll Hall of Fame. It was next door to the science center. Mom and Dad talked to Mr. Peres while we blasted off.

The Rock and Roll Hall of Fame was thermo beyond belief! We saw exhibits about all our favorite rock groups through the ages.

But the Microbe exhibit was the most stellar of all.

Proto Zoa looked so real, I went quasar with excitement! One of my favorite songs was playing. So Neb, Benny, and I danced to the music.

It was truly a Microbe moment.

It had been a thermo trip to Earth. I may not have won the Thirty-Fourth Annual World Science Fair. But my Galaxy Glue had played an important part. And for that, I was proud.

Mom and Dad did punish me when we got back to Space Station 9. No 3D-TV or trips to the Mars Malt for an entire month!

But I had many other stellar things to keep me busy. After all, the *Sixth* Annual Quantum Elementary School Science Fair was less than a year away!

11
ZENON'S GUIDE TO SPACE STATION SLANG

These are some of the terms you'll hear when you visit me on Space Station 9:

Alfred Geezle
He is a 21st-century designer of everything from the clocks on our walls to the treads on our shoes.

blabberbabbles
This is what my friends and I call people who talk too much. This can be an inky thing if it's something you don't want your parents to know about.

Blotozoid Zombie
This is a character from one of the scariest movies I have ever seen,

The Night of the Blotozoid Zombies! It is a very pale creature that slumps forward when it walks. Yuck!

Calzon glass
Although this glass is clear, it has flecks of stardust in it. When you shine a light on it, the stardust glitters and glows.

Ceedus-Lupeedus!
This is our favorite thing to say when we are surprised by something we see or hear.

chill chamber
This is a place, like the Mars Malt, where we go to relax.

cool your boosters
This means you need to calm down and take it easy. I have a hard time with this one.

cosmic
This is when something is out of this world.

data pads
These are our portable computers.

Fenebula
This is the most distant galaxy our scientists have been able to identify.

flared-up
You're flared-up when you're upset and angry. Sometimes your face can turn as red as a solar flare, too.

Flooton plastic
This is the toughest plastic in the universe. It was invented in 2029 by Everett Flooton.

frackles
This is what we call our money. Dad has a hard time parting with his.

geezle bumps
Although these are like goose bumps, we call them geezle bumps.

They look like the treads on the bottoms of the shoes we wear, which were designed by Alfred Geezle.

global meltdown
You go into this when you get upset and lose control of yourself.

inked-out or **inky**
This is when you're spooked or scared.

jet-packs
Jet-packs are fastened behind your back like backpacks. They are filled with fuel and are operated by hand controls so that you can fly around in a zero-gravity bubble when you are playing spaceball.

Jupiter Jell-O
I love this Jell-O! It has a ring around it like Jupiter. The ring is made up of whambama pudding.

Lootar
See Pandorian Lootar.

lunar
(as in "going lunar")
This is the same as going crazy.

Martian mist
When your mind is kind of foggy and confused,
you're in a Martian mist.

Microbe moment
This is a really wonderful moment in time.

Pandorian Lootar
This is a huge monster in a 3-D video
game that we love to play.

Pandorian sunset
This is the most brilliant red sunset in the
universe.

Plutar Blanchy
This is a character from
one of my favorite
children's books,
*It's Not Easy Being a
Plutar Blanchy*. It is a
goofy, easily frightened
creature that walks around
grinning from ear to ear.

Pluto Punch
This is a purple punch as dark as deep space.

quasar
When someone goes quasar, like my dad, it
means that he is very excited because something has made him happy.

scorch
When something is a scorch or scorchy, it's a
bad, bad thing.

shivered-out or **shiver me out**
You get this way when something or someone really gives you the creeps.

spaceball
This is a team game played by hitting a ball back and forth over a net with your hands. It is played in a zero-gravity bubble.

stellar
If something is stellar, it is the most wonderful thing you can imagine!

supernova
(as in "going supernova")
If you go supernova, you become very upset. It's kind of like going into global meltdown.

swallowed up by a black hole
You can feel like you've been swallowed up by a black hole when you feel really bad about something.

thermo
This is something hot, hip, and stellarly cool!

3D-CD & 3D-TV
Not only can we hear our music, but we can see it as well. Our musical groups and TV appear in three-dimensional holograms.

whambama
This is a yummy berry that our scientists have created. It is a combination of banana, pineapple, and kiwi fruit—and you can only get it on Space Station 9!

Whambama Smoothie
No one loves this milk shake more than I do! It's made from whambama berries and ice cream.

Zarkon metal
This is a heavy, dark metal that was discovered by a scientist named Bud Zarkon. It's used in making robots. It can also be used in making clothing, jewelry, and even dog collars.

BUD ZARKON

ABOUT THE CREATORS

MARILYN SADLER and **ROGER BOLLEN** have been creating children's books for over twenty years. Their best-selling titles include the Alistair series of books and the P. J. Funnybunny books, published as Beginner Books by Random House. Their many awards include the International Reading Association Classroom Choice Award and a *Parents' Choice* Award.

Marilyn and Roger originally created Zenon for a hardcover picture book. Then, in January 1999, Disney Channel produced *Zenon, Girl of the 21st Century* as a ninety-minute live-action film. It became the #1 most popular original television movie that year for the channel. This has led Disney to create a second Zenon television movie, *Zenon: The Zequel*, which debuted in January 2001 and was the highest-rated movie in Disney Channel's history.